The Moon in the Pond

Written by Chris Powling

Illustrated by Jeannie Winston

OXFORD
UNIVERSITY PRESS

It was night time. Rabbit, Fox and Bear were sitting by a deep pond.

"Shall we go fishing?"
said Rabbit.

"Fishing?" said Fox.
"In the dark?" said
Bear.
"Look at the moon,"
said Rabbit.

The moon was so big
and so round it lit up
the pond like daytime.

"See?" said Rabbit.
"We can fish till the
sun comes up."

Fox and Bear agreed. Rabbit grinned as they all went to fetch their fishing stuff, but he hid the grin with his paw.

He was playing a trick
on Fox and Bear.

Soon they were back at the pond. Now they had rods and lines and a big, big net.

"Let's start!" said Fox and Bear.

"Wait!" Rabbit yelped. "Look! I can see the moon in the pond! It must have dropped out of the sky."

"Is it sinking?" Fox asked.
"Will it drown?" asked Bear.
"Not if we save it," said Rabbit.

So they fished and fished
and fished.

Yet the moon still gleamed
in the pond.

"We must use our big, big net," said Rabbit at last.

"If I stay on the bank I can show you where to dip. You two must get in the pond close to the moon," he told them.

15

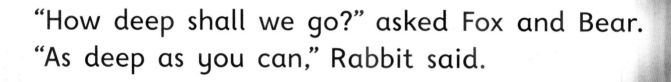

"How deep shall we go?" asked Fox and Bear.
"As deep as you can," Rabbit said.

Fox and Bear splashed into the pond. They flung the net this way and that.

Soon they were soaked from top to toe.
But they still did not save the moon.

"I'm wet all over!" Fox
yelled.
"I'm cold all over!"
added Bear.
"Oh dear ..." Rabbit said.

He jabbed his paw at the sky.
"The moon was up there all along.
It was not in the pond at all."

"ATCHOO!" sneezed Fox and Bear loudly.
"Sorry!" Rabbit called out.

Yet he was not sorry at all. Not when his trick had worked so well.

Rabbit was still grinning when the sun came up and Fox and Bear were still sneezing and cross.

Retell the story

Once upon a time...

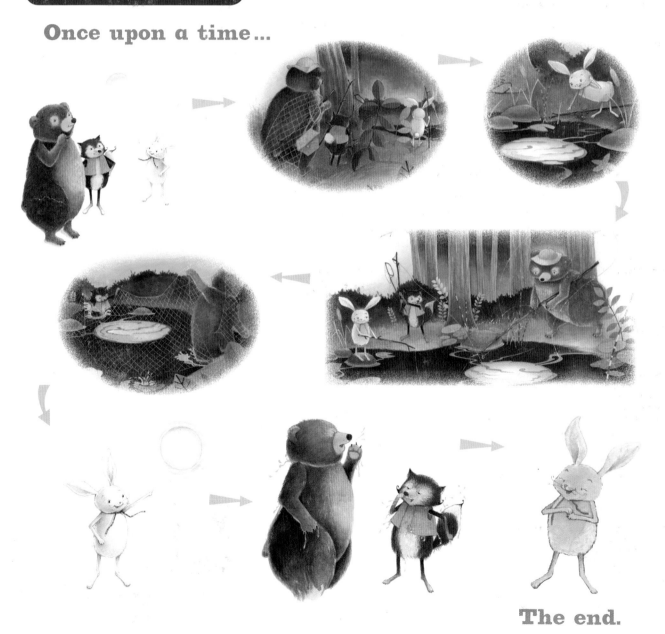

The end.